THE TAILOR SHOP AT THE INTERSECTION

TEXT AND ILLUSTRATIONS BY

AHN JAESUN

TRANSLATED BY
SORA KIM-RUSSELL

Transit Children's Editions

Back in the days of long, fluttering dopo robes, a tailor opened a suit shop at the three-way intersection downtown.

Soon the whispers began.

"What on earth is a suit?"

"They say it's what Westerners wear."

"Why do they wear leashes around their necks?"

"They look so spooky dressed all in black."

採寸

The owner of the shop was Deokgu. With his quick eye and
skilled hands, Deokgu had taught himself how to make suits.
Regardless of what others thought, Deokgu loved the sharp,
clean lines of a suit.

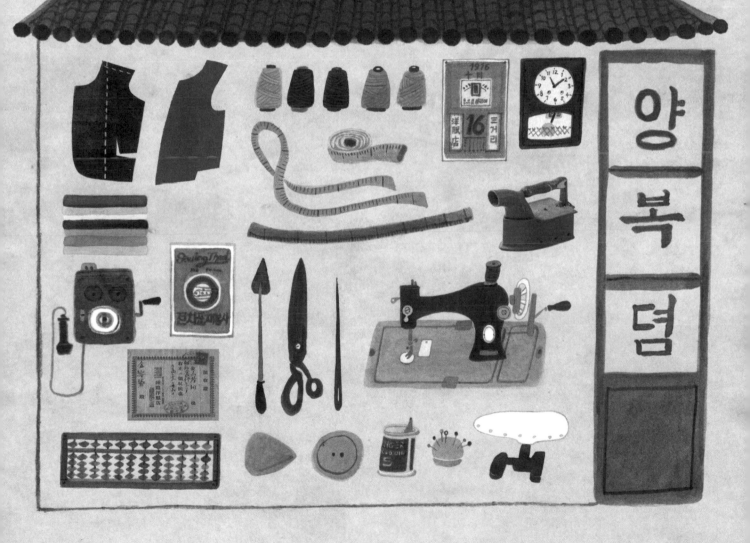

At last, his first customer!
He had never worn a Western
suit before, and Deokgu was
excited to make him a perfect
bespoke suit.

He selects
the right fabric...

Hm, your right arm is shorter than your left.

...and carefully takes his customer's measurements.

Skillfully, he cuts the pattern,

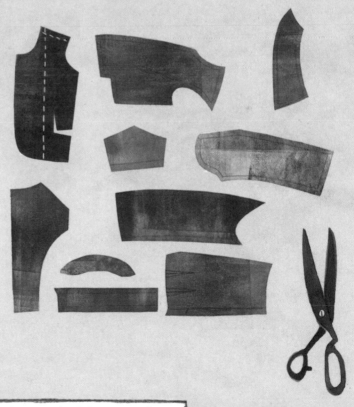

and trims the fabric exactly to size.

He is swift with the machine...

WHIRRR

After pasting the pieces together, Deokgu adds a pin here, swipes some chalk there, until it fits the customer perfectly.

...and precise with every last stitch of the needle. He does it all with great care.

삼거리 양복점 1916

He adds matching buttons and a *Tailor Shop at the Intersection* label,

TSCHHH

and with a few swipes of his charcoal-heated iron, the suit is complete!

Now, this was worth waiting for!

One day, two days, three days, four days...
   A full ten days and still another eight days later, Deokgu's hand-crafted suit was ready.
   When Deokgu saw that his customer was satisfied, he thought to himself, "I'm so glad I became a tailor."

Ahem!

The Tailor Shop at the Intersection makes the best school uniforms, too.

"What on earth is he wearing?"
"What? He looks good!"
Everyone reacted differently at first, but Deokgu's skill was undeniable.
Word got around, and soon every dapper dog had to have their own suit from the Tailor Shop at the Intersection.

I'm the sharpest dresser around.

Then, one day, war swept the land.
   Deokgu returned to the ruined intersection
and got to work rebuilding his shop.

Daddy, what
happened
to our store?

The new owner of the Tailor Shop at the Intersection was Deokgu's third son, Samdol. Samdol took after his father, worked hard, and had a knack for tailoring suits.

삼거리양복

1959

"You have to pour your whole heart into tailoring.
Even the slightest slip will show."
Samdol's father taught him everything he knew, and
now Samdol was waiting quietly for his own customers.

At last, the time had come for Samdol
to show off what he had learned.

1976

Cut by cut and
stitch by stitch,

carefully and
precisely,

just as his father
taught him.

Ten days passed, then another five,

and at last the suits were complete.
Samdol's suits were every bit as good as
his father's. His customers were delighted
at their stylish transformations.

My shop's getting
nothing but flies.

Other tailor shops began to appear at the intersection.
But Samdol's shop was the most popular by far.
All of Samdol's customers said, "Their suits feel like
a second skin."

Soon, suits were being worn for all important
occasions, both happy and sad.

And the Tailor Shop at the Intersection was
there to help.

When Samdol saw this change, he thought
to himself, "It was worth becoming a tailor."

첫돌記念
1
9
7
6.
3.
4.

Many years passed.
The Tailor Shop at the Intersection's
regulars were now old and gray.

VROOM!

Busy, so busy!

The intersection was changing, too.
  New roads were built in mere days, tall buildings in mere months.
  People began to buy cheap, ready-made suits from factories.
  Identical, cookie-cutter suits filled the intersection.

Samdol's second son, Dushik, became the third owner
of the Tailor Shop at the Intersection.

He continued to make custom suits, like his father
and his grandfather before him.

The tools that they had handed down to him were
now quite old.

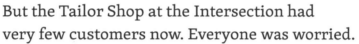But the Tailor Shop at the Intersection had
very few customers now. Everyone was worried.
  "Dushik, you should switch to machine-made
suits instead."
  "You could be churning out three or four suits
in a single day."

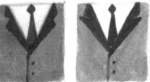

Dushik realized the importance of change.
  But there was one thing he did not wish to change.
  Even if it were quicker and easier, he refused to
work like a machine, churning out identical suits,
made without care.

New customers flocked to the Tailor Shop
at the Intersection.
   Compared to his grandfather and
his father…

Will it fit me?

Of course.

How about this fabric? It's new.

Ooh.

more open to new styles,

I wore this suit the day I met my wife.

and sewed each stitch with great care,

I'll make it like new again.

Dushik was even more precise,

to create a one-of-a-kind suit for each and every customer.

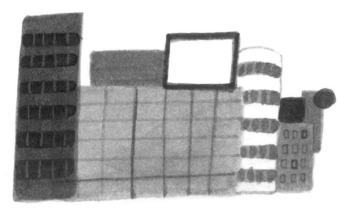

"Only the Tailor Shop at the Intersection can make such unique suits."
When Dushik saw how satisfied his customers were, he thought,
"I'm so happy I became a tailor."

My lady...

What a dapper grandpa!

A measuring tape that never falls short.
Scissors that never cut more than they should.
Needle and thread to stitch together even the smallest of fabric.
An iron to smooth every wrinkle.

A single suit contains the lives of the person who makes it and the person who wears it.

The Tailor Shop at the Intersection has been passed down hand to hand, stitch by stitch, from Grandfather Deokgu's heartfelt care in every piece of fabric to Father Samdol's hard work in every precise snip of the scissors to Dushik's innovations with every stitch and drop of sweat. Crafting suits unique and tailored to every individual…

TSCHHHH

...the Tailor Shop at the Intersection
is still open for business.

Dad!

I always thought it would be wonderful to have a favorite place that I could go back to again and again with my two sons, and with their children as well in the future. *The Tailor Shop at the Intersection* was inspired by that idea. – Ahn Jaesun

The Tailor Shop at the Intersection received the Bologna Ragazzi Award—Opera Prima, Special Mention.

Published by Transit Children's Editions
An imprint of Transit Books
1569 Solano Ave #142, Berkeley, CA 94707
www.transitbooks.org

The Tailor Shop at the Intersection
Originally published in Korea as 삼거리 양복점
Text and illustrations copyright © Jaesun Ahn, 2019
Copyright © 2019 Woongjin Thinkbig Co., Ltd
English translation rights arranged through S.B.Rights Agency—
Stephanie Barrouillet on behalf of Woongjin Thinkbig Co., Ltd
English translation copyright © Sora Kim-Russell, 2023
ISBN: 9781945492761. Library of Congress Control Number: 2023932084.

Design and typesetting by Lawrence Kim

Printed in Italy

9 8 7 6 5 4 3 2 1